Disney
Winnie the Pooh

It's Fun to Learn

A Tiggerific Band

It was a gray day in the Hundred-Acre Wood, but Pooh and his friends didn't mind. There were plenty of things they could do indoors—the problem was, they couldn't think of any!

"Perhaps a little smackerel of something would help," offered Pooh.
And with that, Pooh began searching through his cupboards for a nice, full jar of honey.

"I'll help you look," volunteered Roo. He stuck his head inside a small cabinet and began to rummage around.

"Hooray!" cried Roo suddenly.

Pooh looked hopeful. "Honey?" he asked.

"Something better," answered Roo. He held up two pot lids, then hit them together. "Clangety-clang!" squealed Roo. "Cymbals sure are fun to bang!" He grinned and added, "But Mama says they're only fun if I bang them outside!"

"Say!" cried Tigger. "How about we make a band?"

"But where will we get the instruments?" wondered Piglet.

"We can make them out of all sorts of things," Christopher Robin explained, "just like Roo made cymbals out of pot lids."

"Listen," he said. Christopher Robin picked up an empty honey jar and a spoon. "Rat-a-tat-tat!" he sang. "I made a drum—imagine that!" He circled the room, marching to the beat.

In the meantime, Pooh had finally found a full jar of honey. After taking a quick taste, he announced, "I think I shall play a honey pot, too."

But instead of hitting the pot with a spoon, Pooh began to shake it instead.

"Look! A maraca!" Pooh shouted. But the honey didn't shake, it sloshed—all over poor Pooh!

"Silly old bear," said Christopher Robin gently. "Perhaps you should try an instrument that's a little less messy."

Piglet was having better luck. He'd found a very small jug just right for a very small animal. When he blew across the opening at the top, it made a pleasing whistling sound.

"Toot, toot, toot! My jug sounds like a flute!" Piglet shouted. The music was cheerful—just like Piglet. He danced around Pooh, trying to get him to skip along. "What bad luck," said Pooh. "I think I'm stuck."

Tigger thought he might like to play the jug, too. He picked one up and blew into it. Nothing happened. Tigger tried again, his cheeks as big as balloons. Still the jug was silent. "Tiggers do not like instruments that make them huff and puff!" he declared.

"How about these?" asked Roo, holding out his cymbals.

Tigger crashed the lids together. The loud clanging went into Tigger's ears and echoed around all inside his head. "And tiggers certainly do not like instruments that give them a heady-ache!" he complained.

In the meantime, Pooh had found a wonderful instrument to play. He rattled a jar of buttons. "Shake, shake, shake! That's the sound maracas make!" he chanted.

"Goody!" said Roo. "Our band is almost ready!"

Tigger hung his head. "But there's nothing for me to play," he said sadly.

"We'll help you, Tigger," said Christopher Robin. "What kind of an instrument did you have in mind?"

Tigger thought for a moment. "One that's . . . tiggerish!" he declared.

The friends looked from the top of Pooh's house to the bottom. Surely there was something that Tigger could play.

Roo found two sticks for Tigger to bang together. "Too clicky-clacky," Tigger complained.

Piglet gave him a fireplace fan to squeeze. "Too squeezy-wheezy," decided Tigger. Finally, Pooh gave Tigger his doorbell. "Too ding-a-lingy," said Tigger. He flopped in a chair. "Maybe there's no such thing as a tiggerish instrument," he said with a sigh.

Suddenly Christopher Robin smiled. "Maybe there is something for you, but it just hasn't been invented yet!" he said. "Wait right here!"

Soon Christopher Robin pulled his wagon up to Pooh's house. His friends came out to see an odd collection of junk in the wagon. There were old toys and broken bits and pieces of this and that.

"The only way to make an instrument fit for a tigger is for a tigger to make it himself!" Christopher Robin explained.

Tigger was filled with excitement. "Well, what am I waitin' for?!" he shouted. "I've got work to do!"

Tigger immediately set to work. He grabbed a horn and slung a washboard on his back. Some of his instruments were too heavy to lift, and some made him twist like a pretzel when he played. He looked at the pile of odds and ends in the wagon, trying to decide what to do next.

Roo wanted to make Tigger feel better. "It's okay," he said. "We don't have to make a band. We could just play games instead." Roo picked up a slingshot and an acorn and ran to the nearest tree. *Boing*, went the slingshot.

"That's it!" Tigger cried.

In a few minutes Tigger had built himself a brand-new instrument. When he plucked its slingshot strings, a smile spread across his face.

"Boing, boing! Whee!" exclaimed Tigger, bouncing with glee. "This music sounds just like me!"

At long last the band was ready to play. Each band member took a turn leading a song. Roo started them off with a nice, loud one. Christopher Robin played a rousing tune just perfect for marching. Piglet's song had everyone skipping about, and Pooh's shaker got his pals wiggling and giggling.

When it was Tigger's turn to lead, he even sang a little tune:

> Round and round and do-si-do!
>
> Music makes me tap my toe!
>
> Grab a partner! Feel the beat!
>
> Music gives me happy feet!

Everyone danced and had a wonderful time. But no one had a better time than Tigger, who finally felt the music inside and out!

Fun to Learn Activity

What do ya know! Making a band was a tiggerific idea! Bounce back through the story and try to imitate the sounds our instruments made!

Try your hand at playing a new instrument. How does playing and listening to music make you feel?